RINGO, BOO AND THE MAGNIFICENT 7

ISBN: Paperback: 978-1-80227-099-0
eBook: 978-1-80227-100-3

RINGO, BOO AND THE MAGNIFICENT 7

Neale Paterson

THIS BOOK IS DEDICATED TO

Ringo and Boo, two amazing
Barn Owls and their owlets.

The real Mr and Mrs. W and their wonderful
daughter Harriet, they know who they are.

Also Mrs. P, for letting me spend all my time at the
Kitchen table, pen or paintbrush in hand.

Thanks for believing in a mad idea!

CHAPTER 1

I t was a lovely sunny day at the end of spring. Mr and Mrs
Wood, the owners of Laurels Wood, were sat at the kitchen
table, enjoying a nice hot cup of tea and a cheeky Jammie
Dodger.

They were talking about thing's that parents talk about, when
their young daughter, Harriet, came flying in.

"Mum, Dad, where's Grandad's box of thingies?"

"In the cupboard under the stairs," they both replied. Before they
could ask why, Harriet was off like a mouse scurrying back to the
undergrowth. They both looked at each other in confusion and
decided to see what she was up to.

Just as they got to the bottom of the stairs, Harriet appeared
from the cupboard under the stairs holding her grandad's
binoculars.

"What do you want those for?" asked Mrs W.

"Come and see!" Harriet replied, as she dashed up the stairs to her bedroom.

When they both got there, Harriet was looking out of her bedroom window.

"Look Mum, look Dad, there are two owls in the tree by the barn. Look!"

Mr and Mrs W took it in turns to have a look and to their amazement there in the tree by the old barn were two beautiful barn owls.

"I'm calling them Boo and Ringo," shouted Harriet with glee. Both Mr and Mrs W smiled to each other as Harriet continued to watch the barn owls with excitement.

"Why are you calling them Boo and Ringo?" Mrs W asked.

"If you look closely one has a ring on its leg, and the other is so white that when he flies off, he reminds me of a ghost." Mr and Mrs W both laughed.

Then they left Harriet to enjoy watching Boo and Ringo, the barn owls.

CHAPTER 2

Whilst all the excitement was going on inside Mr and Mrs W's House, the two barn owls were also excited.

"So what do you think? Will it be ok?" Boo asked, as they looked at a gap in the wall of the barn.

"Isn't that where Mr and Mrs Crow live? They're so mean! Always chasing us whenever we get too close," replied Ringo doubtfully, remembering being chased by Mr and Mrs Crow and their four unruly sons when all she was doing was hunting for mice.

"Not anymore! I watched them move out a couple of days ago. I've had a sneaky peek and it would be perfect," exclaimed Boo with a grin on his beak.

"Ok let's go and have a look, but if they come back, no mouse supper for you!" exclaimed Ringo.

With that they both took to the air and gracefully swooped down for a look. Ringo was the first to tentatively stick her head through the hole in the wall.

To her absolute shock it was perfect. She smiled at Boo. "Yes I think this will be just right".

She hopped in for a better look, closely followed by Boo.

Ringo slowly looked around the nest box turning her head, bobbing it up and down.

Boo watched on nervously, hopping from foot to foot, not sure if Ringo really liked it.

"I think we are going to be very happy here Boo," Ringo smiled at Boo.

At least Mr and Mrs Crow and their sons hadn't wrecked the nest box, thought Ringo, quietly surprised.

"Did you see that, Mum? They've both gone into the barn. Do you think they are going to live there?" squealed Harriet with delight.

CHAPTER 3

The following morning Harriet leapt out of bed, excited to get back to her owl watching.

She had perched herself on top of her toy box, and was using her dressing gown folded into a perfect square to use as a cushion to stop her bum from going numb.

After half an hour, and with Mrs W calling Harriet for breakfast, she gave up; not a single owl was to be seen.

During her breakfast of toast and strawberry jam, that Mrs W had made and was Harriet's favourite, Harriet looked to her mum between mouthfuls of toast and exclaimed.,

"I don't think Ringo and Boo have moved into the barn. I looked before breakfast and there was no sign of them. I was so hoping they would move in." Mrs W smiled at her daughter as she did the dishes.

"Owls are nocturnal so they sleep during the day and come out to play at night," explained Mrs W.

"That's not fair! Why can't I sleep in the day and play at night like Ringo and Boo? Then I could watch them playing from my bedroom window. Couldn't? Couldn't I, mum?" exclaimed Harriet.

Mrs W looked at Harriet just as Mr W walked in and said, "Well, if it is ok with your Dad, you can stay up a little bit later tonight and maybe you will see the barn owls coming out." Mr W nodded in agreement.

"Yippee!" shouted Harriet as she scurried off upstairs to get ready, grabbing some snacks as she went.

Later that evening, sat on her toy box with binoculars in one hand and a half-eaten chocolate bar in the other, Harriet spotted Ringo poking her beak out of the hole in the barn, then out she hopped quickly followed by Boo.

They both perched on the ledge just outside. Boo made a loud screech and flew straight up into the air, circled and disappear into the darkness. Ringo seemed to be looking around, bobbing her head up and down almost as if she was doing a crazy little dance. Then, to Harriet's surprise and amazement, she turned her head all the way round. Harriet was shocked and tried turning her head, but it didn't turn as far as Ringo's.

When she looked back Ringo was flying off in the distance. Harriet waited and waited for their return.

When Mr W came to let Harriet know it was time for bed, he found her asleep with her head resting on the window and the binoculars still in her hand, so he gently lifted her up and put her to bed.

CHAPTER 4

During the night Ringo and Boo made themselves busy flying in and out of their new home making everything just so, ready for their special day. They tidied and they hunted. It was going to be a busy time when the new owlets arrived.

Boo returned to find Ringo snuggling down and looking all fluffed up. Ringo smiled a beaky kind of smile, lifted her wing, and to Boo's amazement there was one shiny perfect egg.

"Can I get you anything? Are you ok?" he asked.

"I would love a juicy fat mouse for my tea. This egg laying is hungry work!" Ringo replied

Boo leapt out of the barn to return ten minutes later with the fattest juiciest mouse he could find.

Ringo swallowed it whole.

The next night he dropped another mouse in front of Ringo who lifted her wing. Boo jumped back and counted the eggs – 1, 2.

And so this went on until on the tenth night Ringo lifted her wing to reveal another egg.

Boo scratched his head and counted them again 1, 2, 3, 4, 5, 6. And as if by magic another egg appeared; 7 shiny perfect eggs. Ringo looked up to Boo and in a tired yawn exclaimed, "I think we are going to be rather busy soon," and let out a

little laugh, as she saw the look of total disbelief on Boo's face. Boo snuggled down next to Ringo and they both went to sleep exhausted from all the night's excitement.

Later, they were woken by the sound of the barn doors creaking open and a little voice squealed.

"Yuk! Spider's webs! I hate spiders!" Harriet looked up to the ceiling of the barn to see a big nest box.

"So that's where they are. It's okay, I'm glad you've come to live with us. I'm Harriet by the way," Harriet called, as she peered through all the cobwebs. With the sun shining through the window, it looked like an explosion in a candy floss factory. No one has cleaned in here for a while, Harriet thought to herself, as she went back to the house. The thought of all those spiders gave her the shivers.

The barn doors squeaked closed and Ringo and Boo feel back to sleep.

CHAPTER 5

Over the next few weeks Harriet watched the comings and goings of Ringo and Boo, flying in and out of the nest box every evening.

The first time she saw Boo with a big juicy mouse for Ringo, she thought it was yukky. But over time she had got used to it. Mr & Mrs W had explained to their daughter that's what owls did. So every evening she would count the mice they brought back.

"Mum did you know Ringo and Boo have brought nearly 40 mice back! There can't be many mice left in the fields," she said with a grin on her face.

"I wish I could see what was going on in there." Mr and Mrs W both looked at each other and Mr W gave a thoughtful smile to Mrs W.

That weekend Harriet and her mum went to the park. As they returned, Harriet could see her dad talking to the postman. Mr W had a big parcel in his arms which sparked Harriet's interest.

"Hi Pat!" Harriet shouted out to the postman as she ran past him to catch up with her dad. She always got a chuckle from their postman being called Pat.

"Dad what have you got there? Can I see?"

Mr W laughed. "You'll have to wait and see," he said, and headed off towards the barn.

Harriet turned to her mum. "What's dad doing? Can I go and see? Why's he going to the barn?"

"Questions, questions. If you put your wellies on you can go and help your dad," Mrs W said with a big grin.

Harriet threw her wellies on and ran as fast as her little legs would let her towards the barn.

"Wait for me, Dad! Wait for me!" she was shouting. As she reached the barn Mr W was up a ladder and had a screw driver and some wire, and seemed to be fixing something to the nest box.

"What's that Dad? What are you doing?" Harriet cried impatiently.

"Shhhh! You'll disturb the owls," he whispered. So, Harriet sat in the corner on an old paint can, watching her dad work away.

After ten long minutes her dad climbed down the ladder only to be greeted by Harriet laughing hysterically. "What so funny?" Mr W asked.

"It looks like you're wearing grandad's hair! You're covered in cobwebs!" Harriet replied between giggles". Mr W laughed too, as they both headed back to the house.

CHAPTER 6

To Harriet's delight Mr W had manage to put a camera into the nest box, so hopefully they could watch all the goings on.

Mr and Mrs W, with Harriet, sat in Harriet's bedroom all huddled around a computer screen.

"Are we all ready?" Mr W asked. He switched on the screen and they all gasped. In front of them was a perfect picture of the inside of the nest box, and in the middle were 7 eggs and Ringo fussing about, tidying and pecking around her clutch of eggs.

"We're going to have babies!!!!" shrieked Harriet as she danced around her bedroom and jumped up and down on her bed . . .

They all settled down to watch . . .

Boo returned with another mouse that Ringo gulped down in one go, then settled back down on her eggs.

Ringo suddenly screeched. "Somethings happening, did you hear that?" Ringo lifted herself up and there, sticking out of one of the eggs, was a little pink beak. Both Ringo and Boo screeched a big owl screech with delight. Mr and Mrs W and Harriet all cheered!!

Ringo and Boo both watched as the little owlet broke free from the egg and cried out.

Straight away Boo leapt into action, diving out of the nest box in a cloud of feathers to look for food. When he returned, he was all a fluster, puffing and panting "Got one! I found a small mouse" he said.

Ringo laughed a funny little laugh, as she looked at the panic on Boo's face. She took the mouse and started to feed it to their new bundle of white fluff.

"I'm going to call him Laurel. He looks like a big snowball with big feet" Harriet laughed.

And over the next week or so, all the eggs hatched, leaving a nest box full of Snowballs with big feet.

Harriet named each one as they appeared.

First was Laurel, followed by Bongo, Twilight, Tiny, Luna, Hope and Miracle making up the Magnificent 7 . . .

CHAPTER 7

Ringo was awoken by cries of, "Hungry, Hungry, mummy I'm Hungry". Straight away she knew that was Bongo. Bongo was always hungry; he could demolish at least 5 mice a day, given the chance.

Ringo was ready. Once Bongo started, they all started. "Hurry up Boo," she thought as the screeching got louder. Just in time Boo swooped in with 2 voles and a bat. That should keep them quite for a while.

Bongo jumped to the front of the queue, stepping on Luna's head, who somehow was still asleep in all the commotion. Boo laughed at Bongo who was pulling on the bat's wing, whilst Hope and Miracle looked on at Luna pulling the downy feathers out of Bongos bum for waking her up.

Twilight sat next to Tiny and whispered, "While Bongo is playing with the bat, let's grab a vole each" then came a voice from

behind, "I'm first, I'm the oldest and the biggest," and Laurel dashed passed trying not to trip over Twilight and Tiny.

Whilst Bongo played with his food Ringo shared the voles out between the others. Boo sat there watching and decided to help Bongo, as it looked like the bat was winning the fight. Boo looked at Ringo, who was still busy feeding the other owlets, and asked, "Do you want some of this bat before greedy guts eats it all?" Ringo looked but it was too late. Bongo had already polished it off and was looking for scraps of vole.

"I'll pop out in a bit and find my own, while you look after the kids," she told Boo. As they looked around, all the owlets were curled up and dozing off with fat bellies.

This was now their daily routine. Sleep, eat and repeat. Each day Ringo and Boo saw a difference in their not so little family. Laurel was the leader, Bongo just loved food, Twilight was the quiet one, Tiny, the inquisitive one rummaging around the nest box, Luna, the clumsy one and Hope and Miracle were the mischievous ones.

Harriet loved to watch all the antics at feeding time just before bed, laughing as Hope and Miracle played pranks on all their brothers and sisters. But for all the owlets, their favourite game was to try and catch the spiders. Luna always fell over something, ending up face first in something yukky. Laurel was always stretching and pretending to fly like her mum and dad. Harriet couldn't believe how quickly they were growing, even Tiny. Quite often Mr and Mrs W would join her with a nice cup of tea and a plate of Jammie Dodgers, to watch all the antics as well.

CHAPTER 8

Harriet looked out of her bedroom window, wondering where all the noise was coming from.

It was still early; really early for a Saturday. No one should be out of bed before nine o'clock on a Saturday. As she looked there was a strange man in the garden talking to her Mum and Dad.

Harriet got dressed so fast she nearly forgot to put her socks on, but she needed to find out what was going on in the garden.

As she appeared at the kitchen door, her mum, dad and the strange man were heading towards the barn.

Harriet grabbed her wellies and whilst hopping to put them on, headed down to the barn.

"Morning sleepy head, "shouted Mrs W when she saw Harriet heading towards them.

"What's going on?" Harriet asked, looking at the strange man who had opened the bag he was carrying, to reveal lots of little tools and rings.

"This is Barney Howl. He's come to ring the owlets," Mrs W replied.

"Why do we need to do that?" asked Harriet

"Well Miss, it's so we can identify the owlets and it will help if they get spotted somewhere else. We'll know where they've come from, and how far they have gone from the nest box to start a new life. The same as the mother owl," answered Barney.

"Her name is Ringo" Harriet said looking at Barney.

"Will it hurt them?" Harriet asked.

"Not at all, they'll be fine," replied Barney, reassuring Harriet.

Harriet sat and watched as Barney and her mum got all the owlets from the nest box.

Harriet could hardly contain her excitement as she said hello to each of the owlets and smiled as they looked back, bobbing their heads up and down to see want was going on.
It didn't take long before all the owlets had been ringed and weighed.

Harriet told Barney all their names as he ringed them. "That's Laurel, that's Bongo, that's Twilight, that's Luna, that's Tiny and the last two are Hope and Miracle." As Harriet called out each owlet's name Barney wrote it down in a little book, next to how much each of them weighed.

When it was all done and the owlets were safely back in the nest box, they all headed back to the house for a hot cup of tea and some Jammie Dodgers.

Leaving the owlets to get over all the excitement of the day.

Sitting in the nest box Laurel looked at her leg ring and smiled.

"I look like Mum now I have this ring on my leg," she said, sticking her leg out to admire it, while at the same time kicking Twilight, who was still in shock from the day's events.

All the other owlets agreed that their new leg rings looked rather good. Especially Miracle who loved a bit of bling.

CHAPTER 9

As the week's passed the nest box seemed to get more and more of a squeeze as the owlets grew, thanks mainly to Ringo and Boo's amazing hunting skills. They simply had to keep them all fed.

"Go on I dare you," Shouted Miracle with a cheeky grin. But Laurel ignored her and carried on with her daily wing flapping, bopping Twilight and Tiny on the heads again, as they tried to duck out of the way. "Yeah, go on clever clogs," said Bongo whilst trying to grab another spider snack.

"I could if I wanted to. Look I even have some flight feathers now, so there," scowled Laurel.

All the owlets screeched together, "You're scared". "No, I'm not! I can easily fly up to the gap." And with that Laurel ran towards the gap in the wall, where Ringo and Boo flew out each night

to get food. Wings flapping and leaping into the air, all the owlets held their breath, except for Hope and Miracle who were screeching with glee. Up Laurel went and then with an almighty bang she hit the wall tumbling back down on top of Twilight.

All the owlets except for Luna were laughing. Even Twilight couldn't help but laugh. Luna went over. "Are you ok, Laurel?" she said. All she got in return was a grunt as Laurel went back to wing flapping, trying hard to bop Miracle and Hope on the heads.

"I knew she couldn't do it," laughed Hope. "Maybe we can get her to try again tomorrow. That will be a laugh," chuckled Miracle. "She was quite close. You can see the mark where she hit the wall," added Tiny, and they all fell about laughing again.

Boo's face appeared through the gap. "Who's hungry?" he chuckled, as he dangled a massive rat towards the owlets, knowing Bongo would be first in the queue. After dinner all the owlets settled down for a well-deserved nap.

"I think Laurel was trying to see out of the nest box tonight mum, but she crashed into the wall. It was funny," Harriet told her mum as she was being tucked into bed.

"I don't think it will be long before they are out on the ledge. Now time to go to sleep. Goodnight," said Mrs W before she left Harriet's bedroom.

CHAPTER 10

It wasn't long before Laurel actually made it to the gap after quite a few attempts and being laughed at by the other owlets. Laurel was sure she also saw Boo giggling from a tree opposite when she nearly made it. This just made her even more determined to make it, and finally all the wing flapping paid off.

She proudly perched on the edge of the gap. "I made it," she screeched triumphantly.

"What's out there? What can you see?" the owlets all called out together.

Laurel turned her head back into the nest box and grinned. "Why should I tell you? You all laughed at me."

"Please tell us" pleaded Tiny desperate to know what was outside the nest box. "Please."

"Come on. We won't laugh at you anymore. We promise," added Miracle, also desperate to know.

All the owlets nodded. "Promise!"

Laurel turned back as the others watched, bobbing her head up down, and from side to side. Leaving them all waiting for as long as possible, but she was as excited as the rest of them about what she was seeing. It had taken her days and a few bumps on the head before she finally made it.

"Come on. What can you see," Bongo belched as a spider escaped from his beak. "Aww, now I've lost my snack," Bongo moaned. Laurel ignored the other owlets and tried to take it all in. Laurel was still struggling to focus in the sunlight. The only light they had inside was from the gap where she was now proudly perched. "Move your bum over Laurel, its dark in here. Ouch! I just tripped over Luna," shouted Twilight, not very loudly. But she didn't move. "Do you want me to tell you or not?" Laurel replied.

"Yes we do," said Tiny who was so desperate to find out, he was now hopping from side to side like he needed a wee.

So, Laurel went on to describe the things she could see. Big open fields, lots of flowers swaying in the wind, hundreds of trees all different shapes and sizes, other types of birds flying past, people walking dogs, fields with cows and sheep, a big house with a little girl staring out the window. It was all so much to take in. All the different colours and the wind ruffling her feathers. Laurel thought it was just magical.

Laurel spotted Ringo returning across the fields from a hunt and hopped back in the nest box to cheers from all the other owlets.

CHAPTER 11

Over the next few days, all the owlets attempted to get up to the gap. To everyone's surprise Tiny got the closest, whilst Laurel had perfected getting up to perch in the gap.

Ringo and Boo watched from the tree where Harriet first spotted them both, intrigued as each of the owlets appeared at the entrance to the nest box.

First it was Laurel who was now hopping down on to the ledge, followed by Tiny, Twilight, Luna, Hope, Miracle and finally Bongo who popped through the gap missing the perch and landing in a heap of feathers on the ledge scattering all the other owlets. As they all roared with laughter even Boo and Ringo had a chuckle as Bongo jumped up red faced.

Harriet noticed that Miracle was having trouble getting back up to the entrance to the nest box from the ledge. "Dad, Miracle can't get back in from the ledge. We can't leave her outside all night, she'll get cold." So after more pleading from Harriet, Mr W put on his wellies and coat and headed off to the barn. Luckily there was an old pile of logs just by the side of the barn. Mr W chose a nice log, got his ladder, and climbed up to the ledge where he put the log, so it was easier for Miracle and the other owlets to get back in the nest box. When he returned from the barn Mrs W made him a nice hot cup of tea and gave him a couple of extra Jammie Dodgers, as a reward.

On the ledge Tiny was in his element exploring every little nook and cranny.

Bongo couldn't believe his luck, so many spiders to snack on.

Twilight was amazed by all the different sounds, colours and smells.

Laurel had more space to practice her wing flapping.

Luna stayed away from the edge, because she was the clumsiest and didn't want to fall off. Especially as she didn't have all her flight feathers yet.

Miracle and Hope had managed to find a way to get on the roof of the barn, so they could hide and jump out on the other owlets, which they found hysterical, to the annoyance of their brothers and sisters.

With all the goings on at the barn, now Boo and Ringo seemed to be permanently hunting for voles, mice, frogs, small birds and bats, anything to keep the family fed. It was exhausting work, so as a treat, they would meet at the edge of the woods before going home, and pop to the Owl and Feathers for a quick Vole juice and a pack of deep fried spider's legs. Then they'd head back to see what the owlets had been up to whilst they were out hunting.

"Do you think it will be long before they start to fly?" Boo asked as they soared back to the barn.

"I think Laurel's not far off from fledging, but as for Bongo, if he doesn't stop pinching all the scraps he'll never take off!." They both laughed as they came in to land, to see that all the owlets were fast asleep in the nest box.

CHAPTER 12

All the owlets were out on the ledge enjoying the evening air whilst waiting for Boo to return with their tea. Ringo was also out hunting to help keep the owlets fed.

Laurel, as always, was wing flapping, because she was definitely going to be the first to fly and no-one was going to beat her. As she was practicing, Miracle and Hope were messing about dropping spiders' webs on to Tiny and Luna, when they heard Twilight shout, "Miracle watch out . . . duck".

But before Miracle could react, she was caught on the back of the head by one of Laurels wings and was sent tumbling off the ledge. Luckily, Miracle had been practicing her wing flapping. She flapped for all she was worth, just in time to slow her down before colliding with the ladder Mr W used to put the log up on the ledge for all the owlets. Instead, she ended up in a heap of feathers in the flower beds by the hedge that separated the barn from the fields.

All the owlets were at the edge of the ledge looking for Miracle. "Can anyone see her?" asked Twilight. "She's over there by the ladder," replied Luna.

"What are Mum and Dad going to say? You're in so much trouble, Laurel! Mum's told you about being careful when you're wing flapping," Bongo scoffed. "I'll fly down and rescue Miracle," Laurel said.

"No! Wait for mum and dad! They'll know what to do," Luna replied loudly, which surprised the other owlets.

"Are you okay Miracle?" Hope called out. They all waited and after what seemed like a life time they heard a little voice reply, "I think so. Did you see the way I glided to avoid the ladder? A perfect landing too, apart from a beak full of flowers."

"Do you think you can fly back up before Mum and Dad return?" inquired Laurel.

"I haven't got all my flight feathers yet so I doubt it, but I beat you off the ledge," Miracle laughed a bit nervously. It was then she realised how much trouble she was in.

"Hide under the hedge until Mum or Dad get back," suggested Tiny.

All the owlets looked really worried, especially Hope. "I do hope Miracle's ok," Hope said, looking over the edge.

Then they all noticed the lights come on at the house where the little girl would look from the window just as Bongo threw a snack he had been saving for later, to Miracle.

CHAPTER 13

With all the commotion outside Harriet woke with a start to hear lots of screeching coming from the barn. She jumped out of bed grabbing her grandad's binoculars.

As Harriet focused the binoculars, she could see all the owlets were bobbing their heads up and down as they looked down towards the field.

Harriet counted the owlets 1, 2, 3, 4, 5, 6 . . . One was missing. She counted again. Laurel, Bongo, Twilight, Luna, Tiny and Hope. "Oh no!! Where's Miracle?" Harriet said to herself.

She counted them for a third time. Miracle was definitely missing. She rushed to her computer screen and turned it on. The screen flashed and to her dismay there was no Miracle. "Where is she?" Harriet thought to herself as she ran back to the window. This e as she looked, she noticed all the owlets were looking towards her dad's old ladder. Carefully Harriet focused her Grandad's binoculars, looked all round by the ladder and an old pile of logs, but there was no sign of her. Then out of the corner of her eye she saw something move. It was a little mouse running for safety as Miracle grabbed its tail from her hiding place in the hedge, threw it in the air and gulped it down in one, then hid back in the hedge.

Harriet was so relieved to have found Miracle, but what to do next? Mum and dad were asleep. Should she wake them up?

Harriet threw on her dressing gown, grabbed her torch and headed down the stairs towards the back door. Just as she reached the back door, from behind her she heard footsteps.

A very sleepy Mrs W entered the kitchen. "Harriet why are you up? Where do you think you are going?" she asked as she noticed the torch and that Harriet was now putting on her wellies.

"Mum, Miracle has fallen off the ledge so I'm going to rescue her. I know where she's hiding."

"Okay hold on. Let me get your father and we'll all go and have a look!" Mrs W yawned.

Harriet waited patiently as they all got ready. Slowly creeping down to the barn trying not to trip over tree roots and old logs, Harriet led the way, torch in hand. As they got closer the noise from the owlets stopped, as they all watched Harriet and her parents.

Harriet got down on her Knees and whispered, "It's okay. We aren't going to hurt you. We're here to help". Miracle turned her head and looked at Harriet and recognised her as the girl at the window.

Very slowly Harriet moved her hand forward, waiting to be pecked but to her surprise Miracle didn't put up a fight and just sat in her hands, bobbing her head and looking all around, as Mr and Mrs W got the ladder and rested it on the ledge. For some reason Miracle felt safe with Harriet and knew she wasn't going to hurt her.

All the owlets held their breath as they watched what was happening. "Don't you hurt Miracle!" shouted Hope. As the ladder rested on the ledge all the owlets shuffled away, but stayed on the ledge to see what would happen to Miracle.

Harriet handed Miracle to Mr W and he climbed up to put Miracle on the ledge, and slowly climbed back down, only to fall off the ladder when all the owlets screeched, "HOORAY!! Miracle's safe!"

It made him jump, so he missed the last 2 steps and ended up in a heap, exactly in the same place that Miracle had crash landed.

"Are you okay Dad?" Harriet asked, as Mrs W pulled the ladder off of him.

"Nothing a nice cup of tea and a plate of Jammie Dodgers won't fix, and a good night's sleep," he laughed as they headed back to the house. "I think that's enough adventure for one night," Mrs W whispered as she put Harriet back to bed.

CHAPTER 14

When Ringo returned to the nest box with food, the owlets were so excited, all shouting over each other, totally ignoring the food; even Bongo was ignoring his food! This must be serious, thought Ringo.

"You won't believe what's happened, Mum. Miracle fell off the ledge, Laurel pushed her off doing her wing flapping, bopping her on the head. Miracle just missed the ladder and ended up in a pile of feathers by the hedge. The little girl from the window and her mum and dad rescued Miracle and put her back on the ledge, and the little girl's Dad fell off the ladder and . . ." Ringo interrupted Hope.

"Slow down and start again. Slowly now," Ringo said, shocked by what she had heard.

So one by one they recounted the events of the evening.

Hope told how Laurel knocked Miracle off. Laurel just stood in the corner looking very embarrassed,

Twilight told how they spotted Miracle in the hedge, with Tiny interrupting to say, "It was really scary."

Bongo told them how he threw food down from his secret stash (that all the Owlets knew about), just in case Miracle didn't get rescued.

And Luna told them how the little girl, who was very friendly, helped rescue Miracle. Saying she remembered it was the little girl, Harriet, who came and said hello when they all had their leg rings fitted. "She was so nice, and told us we had nothing to be scared of."

Ringo looked at Miracle who was perched next to Laurel, telling her she was ok and not to worry.

Ringo preened every feather and checked Miracle over to make sure she was ok.

"Mum I'm fine, you don't have to fuss. Mum I stopped myself from crashing into the ladder using my wings. Does that mean I'm the first one to fly?" Miracle laughed looking at Laurel.

When Boo returned he was as shocked as Ringo by all the night's commotion. He fed the owlets and told them to settle down and get some sleep as they were probably very tired from all the excitement. It wasn't long before there was the quiet sound of the owlets snoring, dreaming of the evening's antics.

Whilst the owlets slept, Ringo and Boo nipped off to the Owl and Feathers to have a vole juice to help with the shock of the night's events.

CHAPTER 15

In the morning Harriet awoke to the sunlight sneaking into her bedroom through a gap in the curtains.

Getting out of her bed, she remembered the adventures of the night before.

Hoping that Miracle was ok and didn't get into too much trouble with Ringo and Boo, she crossed the room to open her curtains. There was a tapping noise coming from outside. Harriet reached for the curtains and poked her head through the gap, not sure of where the noise had come from.

As she looked out, in the tree outside her bedroom window, sat Ringo and Boo looking back at her. She squealed at the sight of them and they both bobbed their heads.

Harriet threw on her dressing gown, grabbing her trainers as she leapt down the stairs, crashing through the kitchen, nearly knocking her mum over as she passed Mr W a cup of tea.

"Where's the fire!?" shouted Mr W as Harriet disappeared out of the back door and into the garden.

Mr and Mrs W dashed to the kitchen window to see what their daughter was up to. As they looked out Harriet was sat on one of the garden chairs talking to something in the tree. To their amazement in the tree sat Ringo and Boo, looking back at Harriet.

"Is Miracle ok?" Harriet asked. Both Ringo and Boo bobbed their heads. Then Ringo fluffed her feathers and pulled a feather out, leant forward and dropped it. Harriet watched as the feather floated down and landed perfectly in her lap.

Ringo and Boo let out a little screech and flew off towards the barn.

Harriet ran back into the house waving her feather. "Look! Ringo gave me one of her feathers!" she screamed with excitement

Harriet laid it on the kitchen table, and they all had a look. To their surprise the feather was a light brown with beautiful white markings and in the very centre of the feather was a white marking in the perfect shape of a heart.

They all gasped. "I think Ringo and Boo are trying to say thank you for rescuing Miracle," said Mrs W, looking at Harriet and then back at the feather, not sure she could believe what they were seeing.

Harriet run towards the stairs with the feather. "I'm going to treasure this forever," she called out ,before disappearing into her bedroom.

Harriet sat on her bed admiring the feather, looking at the white heart, before placing it under her pillow for safe keeping.

Before bed Harriet looked out to the barn to check on the owlets. She was pleased to see them all on the ledge waiting for Ringo and Boo's return, including Miracle. With a smile she climbed into bed checking the feather was still under the pillow, before drifting off into a blissful sleep.

CHAPTER 16

As the days passed each of the owlets grew in confidence, and as suspected, and through sheer determination Laurel was the first to take the leap of faith, to a round of applause from the other owlets. She soared up into the air shouting, "Look I'm doing it! I'm flying!" before coming back to the ledge to land. Harriet had now named it the fledge ledge.

One by one they all took to the air. Some with more success than others. Tiny was the next to go and also managed to land next to Ringo in the tree opposite the barn, which meant it was somewhere else to explore. Then Luna, who seemed to be naturally soaring higher and higher, before swooping down and across the fields so close to the ground the others could see the flowers moving as she went past.

She screeched, "Yippee" as she passed. Twilight followed, crash landing onto the ledge, much to the amusement of all the others. Bongo was next. He had heard about all the mice in the field behind the barn, so with a big run up he leapt from the ledge then disappeared downwards before soaring over the hedge and out towards the field. He was extremely upset when he returned. He had only managed to catch one mouse and he dropped it before he had the chance to eat it!

That only left Miracle and Hope, who were egged on by the others and their stories about how high they had reached and how they could now catch their own food. Hope just went for it, leaving Miracle to watch as she flew past screeching ,"Come on

Miracle! This is much more fun than chasing spiders or hiding Bongo's food."

Miracle looked over the edge and remembered the day she fell. Luna whispered in her ear, "It will be okay. Remember you were the first to fly." Miracle smiled back at Luna, bobbed her head then looked at the others, who all screeched, "You can do it." With that, Miracle closed her eyes, flapped her wings then leapt into the air. She couldn't feel the ledge under her claws. As she opened her eyes and looked, the barn was below her. Hope swooped past shouting "I told you it was fun."

All the other owlets flew into the air cheering.

Harriet was watching from her window, binoculars in one hand, feather in the other. "I knew you could do it Miracle," she thought to herself with a smile.

CHAPTER 17

ow that all the owlets could fly, they spent a lot less time on the ledge. Instead, they would be out hunting most of the night and only return to sleep in the nest box.

They had all now fledged and were making their own way in the big wide world. Hope and Miracle tended to return more often, perching on the log or the ledge.

Harriet would sit at her window to watch, but she would only get the occasional glimpse when one of the owls was hunting near the barn.

As she sat on her bed, Mrs W came into the bedroom. "If you look outside, I think you have some visitors." Harriet Rushed to her window, jumping over her toy box as quickly as she could.

In the tree outside sat all the owlets. As she looked at each in turn, they bobbed their heads and then flew off. "Goodbye Laurel, Goodbye Luna, Goodbye Twilight, Goodbye Bongo, Goodbye Tiny, Goodbye Hope," Harriet waved as each of them took off, leaving only Miracle behind. Harriet ran back to her bed and grabbed the feather, showing it to Miracle.

The last little owlet bobbed her head, looked back to Harriet and then flew off into the distance. "Bye-bye, Miracle"

Harriet looked back to her mum. "Do you think I will see Miracle again?"

"Let's hope so," replied Mrs W. "Let's hope so," leaving Harriet looking out of her bedroom window, wondering what adventure the owlets would have now that they were gone.

THE END

MIRACLE   TINY   HOPE   TWILIGHT   BONGO   LUNA   LAUREL

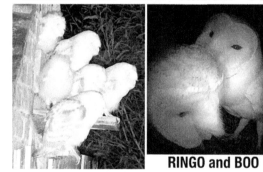

RINGO and BOO